This book is for:

_____

From:

_____

Date:

_____

Christmas in Heaven

Anthony DeStefano
Illustrated by Bernadette Carstensen

SOPHIA INSTITUTE PRESS
Manchester, NH

This book is dedicated to the person most responsible
for helping me to become a committed Catholic
many years ago—my sister, Elisa Fagundes.

—*Anthony DeStefano*

Dedicated to my first and best teachers,
mom and dad—Winifred and Larry Carstensen.

—*Bernadette Carstensen*

SOPHIA
INSTITUTE PRESS

Text Copyright © 2024 by Anthony DeStefano.

Images Copyright © 2024 by Bernadette Carstensen.

Printed in the United States of America.

Sophia Institute Press®
Box 5284, Manchester, NH 03108
1-800-888-9344

www.SophiaInstitute.com

Sophia Institute Press® is a registered trademark of Sophia Institute.

ISBN: 978-1-64413-999-8

Library of Congress Control Number: 2024942017

First Printing, 2024

Note to Readers on Purgatory

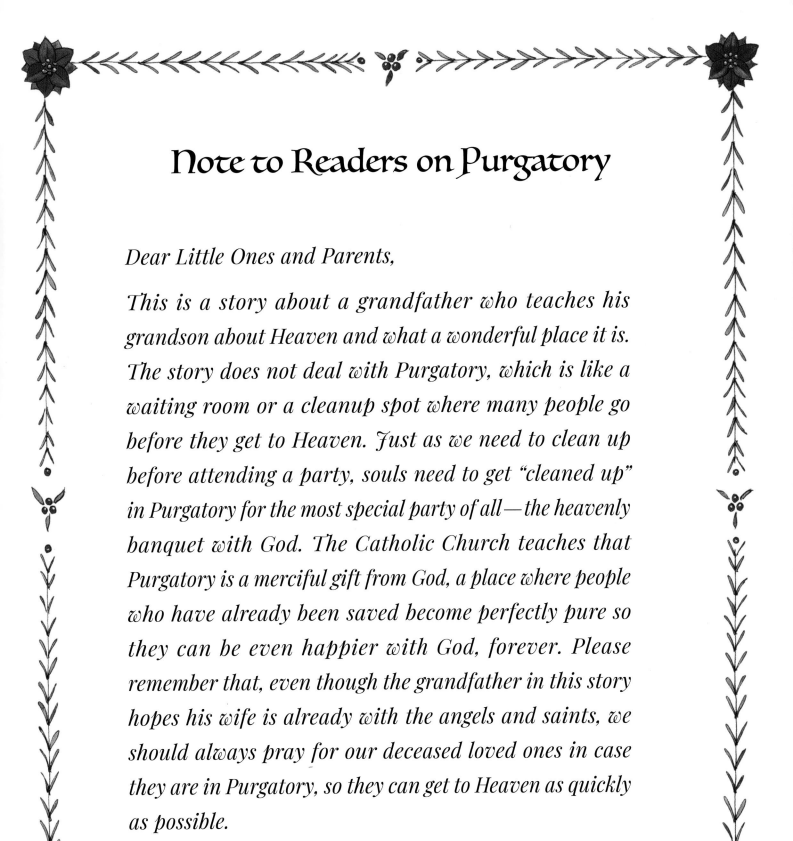

Dear Little Ones and Parents,

This is a story about a grandfather who teaches his grandson about Heaven and what a wonderful place it is. The story does not deal with Purgatory, which is like a waiting room or a cleanup spot where many people go before they get to Heaven. Just as we need to clean up before attending a party, souls need to get "cleaned up" in Purgatory for the most special party of all—the heavenly banquet with God. The Catholic Church teaches that Purgatory is a merciful gift from God, a place where people who have already been saved become perfectly pure so they can be even happier with God, forever. Please remember that, even though the grandfather in this story hopes his wife is already with the angels and saints, we should always pray for our deceased loved ones in case they are in Purgatory, so they can get to Heaven as quickly as possible.

The Author

"How do they celebrate Christmas in Heaven?"
the little boy asked, who was no more than seven.

His grandma had gone to be with the Lord.
He wanted to know if she would be bored
up in the clouds, so high in the sky,
while everyone here just wanted to cry.

His grandfather lifted the boy on his knee.
He said: "Close your eyes and listen to me.

"The reason we celebrate Christmas on Earth
is that it's the day of our dear Savior's birth.

"In Heaven they're having a giant affair.
All of the saints and the angels are there.

"St. Gabriel's starting the big celebration
by blowing his horn in sweet adoration.

"St. Peter is standing outside Heaven's gate
making sure none of the guests have to wait.

"Inside, St. Martha's
been cleaning for hours,
while little Thérèse
is handing out flowers.

"St. Lucy is putting
the lights on the tree,
making it merry
and bright as can be.

8

"St. Joseph, who once saved his family from danger,
is under the Christmas tree building a manger.

"St. Nick is unloading
   the toys from his sleigh,
for all Heaven's children
   on this happy day.

"'I can't find a present,'
   the jolly man shouts.
St. Anthony rushes
   to help the saint out.

"St. Martha stops cleaning
and now starts to cook,
while Thomas Aquinas
sits reading a book.

"St. Lawrence is turning
the roast on a fire,
while Joan of Arc helps him
to make the flames higher.

"St. Valentine has chocolate hearts on a tray.

"St. Martin de Porres helps give them away.

"Cecilia and Gregory sing a duet.
They're joined by two angels to make a quartet.

"St. Luke is there painting
the choir as it sings.
St. Mark flies above
on a lion with wings.

"St. Martha starts dusting
   and sweeping all over.
St. Patrick awards her
   an emerald-green clover.

"And there on the table's a huge birthday cake
that's taken St. Honoré so long to bake.

"St. Matthew's been up counting candles all night.
There's over two thousand St. John has to light!

"All of a sudden, the door opens wide.
In walks St. Francis, and there by his side
are kittens and puppies and donkeys and sheep.
St. Martha is following, trying to sweep.

"'It's hopeless,' she says, 'there's too much to do.'
St. Jude helps her finish—a miracle come true!"

"Oh wow," said the boy, when grandpa was done.
"Heaven's exciting and seems like such fun!

"But wait," the boy asked, attempting to see.
"Where is my grandma? Where can she be?"

"Look over there," his grandfather said.
The boy saw a girl who was sleeping in bed.

"But that's not my grandma—my grandma is old.
That lady is young—her hair is all gold."

His grandfather answered: "You don't understand.
No one is old in this glorious land.
The people in Heaven are all young once more.
They're even more lovely than they were before.
Just look at your grandma! Look at my wife!
The most beautiful person I've known in my life!

"But wait! It's the Lord, whose birthday's today.
He's walking toward grandma; the saints all make way."

27

"The Lord looks at grandma,
   His face is aglow.
He speaks the same words
   that He spoke long ago:

"'Maiden I tell you
   it's time to arise.'
And look! Grandma hears Him
   and opens her eyes!

28

"The Lord takes her hand and leads her to where
St. Michael is waiting to hold out her chair.

"She sits down right next to Our Lady the Queen,
looking more joyful than I've ever seen.

"And now all the angels
and saints start to sing:

'Happy birthday to Jesus!
Happy birthday, Our King!'

"And now grandma spots us—she's waving, you see?
She's blowing some kisses to you and to me!"

Just then the boy felt a warm breeze on his cheek.
He opened his eyes, excited to speak.

"Grandma just kissed me! I felt it! It's true!
She saw us and smiled and waved at us too!"

The grandfather gave the young boy an embrace.
He put him down gently and kissed the boy's face.

"I told you," he whispered, "there's no need to fear.
Don't be unhappy and don't shed a tear.
It's OK that grandma is no longer here.
She's spending her Christmas in Heaven this year."

Glossary of Angels and Saints *(In order of appearance)*

St. Gabriel the Archangel

An archangel known for delivering God's messages, St. Gabriel announced the births of John the Baptist and Jesus Christ. According to tradition, he will blow his trumpet at the end of the world, signaling the resurrection of the dead. He is the patron saint of those who work in the field of communications.

St. Peter

A Jewish fisherman, St. Peter was the leading apostle and the first pope. Jesus' promise to give him "the keys of the kingdom of Heaven" (Matt. 16:19) led to the popular idea that St. Peter is the gatekeeper of Heaven and greets all the souls who enter.

St. Martha

A New Testament figure known for her hospitality toward Jesus and her willingness to work hard, St. Martha is the patron saint of servants, cooks, waiters, and waitresses.

St. Thérèse of Lisieux

A Carmelite nun, St. Thérèse is known for her simple approach to spirituality, called the "Little Way." Her autobiography, *The Story of a Soul*, is one of the bestselling books of all time. St. Thérèse is famous for saying, "I will send down a shower of roses from Heaven." She is the patron saint of missionaries and florists.

St. Lucy

A fourth-century martyr from Sicily, St. Lucy was known for her devout faith in the face of persecution. Before she was killed, her eyes were gouged out. She is the patron saint of the blind and is often associated with light.

St. Joseph

The foster father of Jesus and the husband of the Virgin Mary, St. Joseph was a Jewish carpenter known for his commitment to protecting the Holy Family and for being a just and righteous man. He is the patron saint of fathers, workers, and the universal Church.

St. Nicholas

Known for his great generosity, St. Nicholas was the bishop of the ancient city of Myra in Greece. His life inspired the traditional figure of Santa Claus, and he is the patron saint of children, sailors, and unmarried people.

St. Anthony

A Franciscan priest known for his powerful preaching and knowledge of Scripture, St. Anthony was born in Portugal and later moved to Padua, Italy. He is famous for performing great miracles and is the patron saint for finding lost items.

St. Thomas Aquinas

A thirteenth-century Dominican friar, Doctor of the Church, and one of the Church's greatest theologians, St. Thomas wrote the *Summa Theologica* and is the patron saint of students and universities.

St. Lawrence

A heroic deacon, St. Lawrence was martyred during the third century in the Roman Empire and is famous for being roasted to death on a gridiron. Legend has it that he bravely told his executioners, "Turn me over; I'm done on this side!" He is the patron saint of cooks.

St. Joan of Arc

A national heroine of France, St. Joan believed she was acting under divine guidance when, at age seventeen, she led the French army to a great victory over the English during the Hundred Years' War. She was captured and burned at the stake, but she was eventually canonized and made patron saint of France, soldiers, youth, and those in need of courage.

St. Valentine

A Christian bishop from the third century, St. Valentine was executed by the Romans for illegally marrying Christian couples. He is the patron saint of men and women in love.

St. Martin de Porres

A sixteenth-century Dominican lay brother from Peru, St. Martin was the son of a Spanish nobleman, but his mother was a freed slave of African and native descent. Known for his care for the sick and the poor, he is the patron saint of mixed-race people, racial harmony, and social justice.

St. Cecilia

An early Christian martyr in Rome, St. Cecilia vowed her virginity to God but was forced into marriage. As musicians played at her wedding, she sat apart from everyone and "sang in her heart to the Lord" as a protest. She was soon executed for keeping her vow of virginity. She is the patron saint of musicians.

St. Gregory the Great

A pope during the Middle Ages, St. Gregory was a great theologian and Doctor of the Church. He is credited with developing the beautiful Gregorian chant that for centuries has been sung in Latin by choirs. He is the patron saint of singers.

St. Luke the Evangelist

The author of the Gospel of Luke and the Acts of the Apostles, St. Luke was a companion of St. Paul and was a physician and an artist who, according to tradition, painted the very first portrait of Our Lady. He is the patron saint of doctors and artists.

St. Mark the Evangelist

The author of the Gospel of Mark, St. Mark was a companion of St. Paul. Early Christians used different creatures to symbolize the four evangelists (Matthew, Mark, Luke, and John), and the symbol for St. Mark was a winged lion, which is believed to represent key themes found in his Gospel, such as courage, strength, kingship, and Jesus' triumph over death.

St. Patrick

A fifth-century missionary and bishop who converted Ireland to Christianity, St. Patrick is known for banishing the snakes from the country and for using a shamrock — a three-leaf clover — to explain the mystery of the Holy Trinity.

St. Honoré

A sixth-century French bishop, St. Honoré is celebrated for his great compassion for the poor. Legend has it that after his death, several miracles occurred relating to the wheat harvest and the production of bread. St. Honoré is the patron saint of bakers and pastry chefs.

St. Matthew the Evangelist

Also known as Levi, St. Matthew was one of the Twelve Apostles and the author of the Gospel of Matthew. He was a tax collector before being called by Jesus, and he is the patron saint of accountants, bookkeepers, and bankers.

St. John the Evangelist

Known as the "beloved disciple," St. John is the author of the Gospel of John and the book of Revelation. His Gospel is famous for using light as a symbol and for showing that Jesus is the "light of the world" (John 8:12).

St. Francis of Assisi

Born in Italy in the twelfth century, St. Francis embraced a life of poverty, cared for the poor and the sick, founded the Franciscan Order, received the stigmata (the wounds of Christ on his body), and is known for his great love of animals and of nature.

St. Jude

One of the twelve apostles, St. Jude wrote the Letter of Jude, which stresses the importance of having faith and praying in union with the Holy Spirit. He is known as the patron saint of desperate cases and lost causes because so many people throughout history have prayed to him and received miracles.

St. Michael the Archangel

The leader of God's army of angels, St. Michael defeated Satan and cast him out of Heaven. He is known as a protector against all evil and is the patron saint of the military, police officers, firefighters, knights, and chivalry (polite and honorable behavior, especially by men toward women).

Our Lady, Queen of Heaven

The Blessed Virgin Mary, Mother of Jesus Christ, was assumed into Heaven upon the completion of her life on Earth and was crowned as its queen.

Our Lord, Jesus Christ

Our Lord is neither an angel nor a saint. Rather, He is God Himself. He became a man in the person of Jesus Christ, and His death by crucifixion made it possible for people to go to Heaven and to be happy forever. We celebrate His birth on Christmas.